Enid Blyton's
NODDY
and the Prize Catch

BBC CHILDREN'S BOOKS

It was a thrilling day in Toyland. It was the day of the Toyland fishing contest, and Big-Ears was going to help Noddy buy a new fishing-rod.

"I've never had a fishing-rod before, Big-Ears," said Noddy. "I'm so excited!"

Just then, Mr Plod stepped out in front of the car. "One moment please, Noddy!" he shouted. "I should like you and Big-Ears to help me with my enquiries. Mrs Noah's beautiful ruby ring, the finest ring in Toyland, has disappeared!"

"Oh, dear," said Big-Ears. "Has it been stolen?"

"Very possibly," replied Mr Plod. "If you should find it, there's a reward of four sixpences."

"Four sixpences! I could buy two fishing-rods – one for each hand! We'll certainly look out for it," said Noddy.

Noddy and Big-Ears drove off towards Toy Town. Poor Mr Plod had to jump out of their way quickly, and fell into a large holly bush.

"Ooh! Ow! Dear me!" cried Mr Plod. "I think I've sat on a piece of holly!"

Meanwhile, the two goblins
were making mischief again.

"This ring's worth a fortune,
Sammy Sailor," said Gobbo.

"And you just found it, you say?" asked Sammy.

"Yes, we just found it in the woods," said Gobbo.
"And you can buy it for just six sixpences!"

"I'll take it!" said Sammy. "I can sell a ring like this."

"You mustn't show it to anyone in Toyland," said Gobbo.

"I shall keep it hidden in my sea-chest," promised Sammy, "and I shall hide my sea-chest where no one will think of looking!"

Eventually, Noddy arrived at the seaside shop.

"It's locked!" he said, disappointedly. "The shop's closed. I shan't be able to buy my fishing-rod." Just then, he heard Martha Monkey calling him.

"Hello, Noddy!" she cried. "Have you come to practise for the fishing contest?"

"I'd like to," replied Noddy, "but I haven't got a fishing-rod."

"You don't need a rod," said Martha. "I use my tail. I've already caught one fish. Look, it's in the basket."

Noddy opened the basket sitting next to Martha and there inside lay a fish. It leapt up into Noddy's arms and jumped straight back into the harbour!

"I'm sorry, Martha," said Noddy. "I've lost your fish!"

"It doesn't matter," said Martha. "It's easy to catch more fish when you've got a tail like mine!"

"I wish I had a tail like yours," sighed Noddy.

"You can buy my spare tail," offered Martha.

"I've only got two sixpences," said Noddy.

"This tail costs exactly two sixpences," said Martha. "Just pin it to the back of your shorts and dangle it into the water."

Some time later, Noddy still hadn't caught any fish.
"Martha Monkey's own tail must be a much better
fishing-tail than this one," grumbled Noddy, unhappily.
Mr Jumbo appeared and walked over to Noddy.

"Hello," cried Noddy. "Have you come to practise fishing with your tail?"

"Certainly not," said Mr Jumbo. "A good fisherman uses his trunk. I've already caught one fish." Mr Jumbo looked inside his basket. "Where's my fish?" he cried.

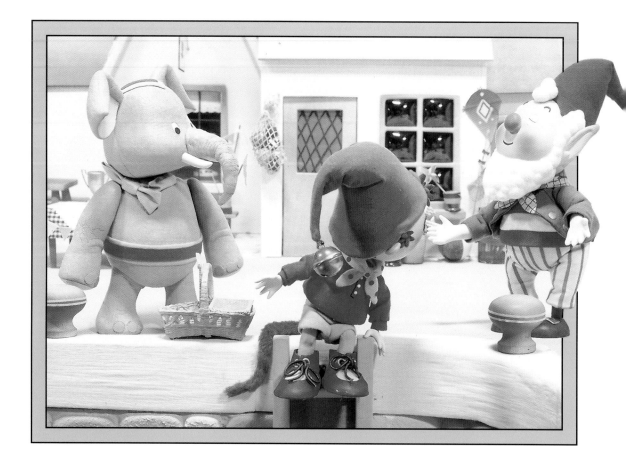

"Your fish?" said Noddy. "Didn't Martha Monkey catch it with her tail?"

"No," said Jumbo. "I caught it, but it's gone!"

"So this isn't a fishing-tail at all," said Noddy. "Martha Monkey played a trick on me."

Just then, Big-Ears arrived. "Dear me, you have got into trouble," he said. "I will *make* you a fishing-rod."

"Oh, thank you, Big-Ears!" cried Noddy.

A little later, Big-Ears finally put the finishing touches to Noddy's new fishing-rod.

"Thank you! It's much better than Martha Monkey's spare tail," said Noddy, happily.

"It's my pleasure," said Big-Ears. "Now, let's set off for the harbour."

Mr Plod was just announcing the start of the fishing contest.

"By popular request," he began, "I have been asked to interrupt my enquiries into the disappearance of Mrs Noah's ruby ring, to declare this fishing contest – open! Whoever catches the greatest weight of fish in one hour will win this silver cup. On your sharks . . . get wet . . . go!"

A minute later, Sammy Sailor arrived at the harbour. He was very surprised to see all the toys fishing there.

"What's going on?" he demanded.

"It's the Toyland fishing contest," replied Mr Plod.

"It can't be! I've come to fish for my . . . er . . . I want to join the contest!" said Sammy Sailor, hurriedly.

"You're very late," said Mr Plod, "but you can fish over at the end of the quay."

"I need to fish next to Noddy," said Sammy, and he rushed over. "Move over, Noddy. I want to fish here."

"It's not a very good spot," warned Noddy. "I've only caught two old boots – and they're not even a pair!"

Sly and Gobbo were hatching a naughty plot over by the harbour steps.

"Quick! No one's looking," said Sly.

"Hee hee! They'll never catch a bigger fish than this!" giggled Gobbo.

"And then that big silver cup will be ours!" tittered Sly.

Gobbo picked up a big fish that he'd bought earlier and handed it to Sly. "Hold tight!" he said.

"Oh, no! Help!" shrieked Sly, as he lost his footing and fell into the water with a very loud splash!

"My word," said Big-Ears. "It sounds like someone's caught a very big fish."

"So have I," said Noddy, as he felt a big tug on his line. "I think I've caught a huge fish."

"Pull hard, Noddy," said Big-Ears, encouragingly.

Noddy heaved and heaved until he pulled in a large, brown chest.

"What a strange-looking fish," said Noddy.

"That's not a fish, Noddy," said Mr Plod. "That's a sailor's sea-chest, isn't it, Sammy?"

"Erm, well, yes, it might be," stammered Sammy.

"There could be treasure inside it!" exclaimed Noddy. He opened the lid and gasped in amazement as he saw the beautiful treasure it held. "It's a ruby ring!"

"Goodness gracious me!" said Mr Plod. "Unless I'm much mistaken, that's the very ruby ring that was stolen from Mrs Noah! I wonder how it got here?"

"I must be going now," whispered Sammy Sailor, as he got ready to creep off.

"One moment, please," said Mr Plod, sternly.

"I have reason to believe that this is indeed your sea-chest, and that you stole Mrs Noah's ruby ring!"

"I didn't!" protested Sammy. "I bought it. I bought the ring from Sly and Gobbo for six sixpences. They said they found it in the woods."

"Stole it, more like," said Mr Plod. "Where are they?"

"They're over there," said Noddy, "and they're taking the silver cup!"

"Hee hee!" snickered Sly.

"Let's get away before they spot us," said Gobbo, as he grabbed the silver trophy.

"Come back!" shouted Mr Plod. "Come back!"

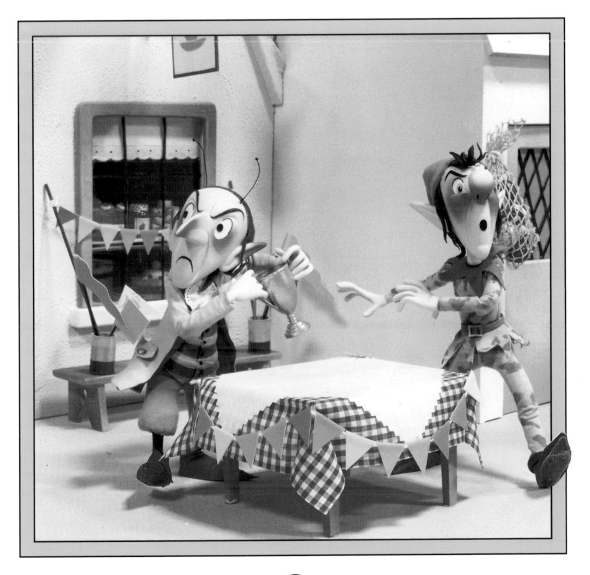

"Don't worry, I'll catch them, Mr Plod!" cried Noddy. He stood up and cast his fishing-line after the two bad goblins. The hook caught the back of Sly's heel.

"Help!" cried Sly and Gobbo, as they went flying. "Ow! Ouch!"

"You goblins are both under arrest!" bellowed Mr Plod.

"Well done, Noddy," said Mr Plod. "You have caught Mrs Noah's ruby ring and the silver cup. As judge of the Toyland fishing contest, I hereby declare that Noddy has made the biggest catch of the day and should therefore receive the silver cup!"

"Hooray!" cheered the toys. "Well done!"

"And he shall receive four sixpences for finding Mrs Noah's ruby ring," added Mr Plod.

"You'll be able to buy a new fishing-rod after all," said
Big-Ears.

"No, Big-Ears – this is the best fishing-rod anyone could
have," replied Noddy. "But I do know how I shall spend
my reward – as soon as we all get back to town, I shall
buy everyone . . . the most enormous . . . fish supper!"

Published by BBC Children's Books
An imprint of BBC Worldwide Publishing
Woodlands, 80 Wood Lane, London W12 0TT

First published 1995
Reprinted 1995

Text and design copyright © 1995 BBC Children's Books
Stills copyright © 1995 BBC Worldwide Publishing

ISBN 0 563 40514 7

Based on the Television series, produced by Cosgrove Hall Films Limited,
inspired by the Noddy Books which are copyright © Darrell Waters Limited 1949– 968

Enid Blyton's signature and Noddy are Trademarks of Darrell Waters Limited

Typeset in 17/21 pt Garamond by BBC Children's Books
Printed and bound in Great Britain by Cambus Limited, East Kilbride
Colour separations by DOT Gradations, Chelmsford